AUTUMN
PUBLISHING

Published in 2022
Published in the UK by Autumn Publishing
An imprint of Igloo Books Ltd
Cottage Farm, NN6 0BJ, UK
Owned by Bonnier Books
Sveavägen 56, Stockholm, Sweden
www.igloobooks.com

© 2022 Disney Enterprises, Inc. All rights reserved.

No part of this publication may be
reproduced or transmitted in any form or by any means,
electronic, or mechanical, including photocopying, recording,
or by any information storage and retrieval system,
without permission in writing from the publisher.

1022 001
2 4 6 8 10 9 7 5 3 1
ISBN 978-1-80368-493-2

Written by Nancy Parent
Illustrated by Jerrod Maruyama

Printed and manufactured
in China

Disney
My First Stories

ELSA TO THE RESCUE

On a sunny **spring** day in Arendelle,
Anna is searching for Olaf. "Hmmm," she
says. "Where can he be?"

When she cannot find him, she asks
Elsa, Kristoff and Sven for help.

Anna and her friends head into the
forest, where they come upon a bear cub.
"Oh, the poor thing," says Anna.

"His paw is **stuck**," says Elsa.
"We've got to help him."
 But as Kristoff approaches the cub,
the young animal shakes and growls.

"I can't get any closer," says Kristoff. "He's too frightened."

So Elsa points at the **large** rock pinning down the bear's paw. When it magically freezes, Kristoff takes a shovel from his wagon and smashes the rock to pieces. The cub is free!

Soon they come upon a **family** that has stopped along the trail.

"Our wagon wheel is broken," says the man.

"I think I can fix it," Kristoff says.
While they wait, Anna asks, "Have you seen a little **snowman**?"

"Sorry, no," says the man. "But I hope you find him. And we thank you for your help."

A **generous** Sven shares his carrots before the family says goodbye.

By nightfall, Elsa and her friends arrive at the trolls' **home**. Kristoff's family welcomes them.

"Why?" asks **Olaf**. "Are we far from home?"

"You could say that," says Anna.

"Maybe this will make it worth the trip," says Olaf as he hands bouquets to Anna and Elsa. "Sorry, Sven and Kristoff!"

As the wagon approaches **Arendelle**, Anna points out all the flowers that grow close to the castle.

"Look, Olaf," says Anna. "Next time you won't have to go **so far** to pick them!"

"Has anybody seen Olaf?" asks Kristoff. "We've been looking for him all day."

The trolls all shake their heads and shrug. Then the youngsters surround Kristoff. "How about a quick game of **Troll Rolling** before you leave?" a young troll asks.

Soon it's time to say **goodbye**!
As they ride through the forest, Kristoff sees
some wolves out prowling.

"Hurry, Sven," says Kristoff. "Let's go!"

The wagon soon comes to a stop in front of a **ravine**. Elsa uses her magic to create an ice bridge. The wagon slides across quickly, leaving the wolves behind.

In the dark distance, they see a **familiar** white shape picking wildflowers.

"Hello!" the shape calls, running towards them. "Are you here to collect **flowers**, too?"

"Actually," says Elsa, "we've come to collect you!"